All the sugar on Earth has been stolen — to make energy for other planets light years away. Professor Gamma pursues the thief across the energy pathways of the universe to put matters right.

To Christina

Titles in Series 823
The Energy Pirate
The Frozen Planet of Azuron
The Giants of Universal Park
The Planet of Death

First edition

© LADYBIRD BOOKS LTD MCMLXXXII

THE ENERGY PIRATE

by Fred and Geoffrey Hoyle
illustrated by Martin Aitchison

Ladybird Books Loughborough

The Energy Pirate

It was pocket-money day, and William kicked idly at stones on the edge of the road outside the village shop. He'd come to buy his weekly Neutron Chocolate Bar, and the shop was closed, which puzzled him because normally it would have been open by now. A small delivery van from the Neutron chocolate factory stood unattended close by.

William kicked hard at another stone and watched as it careered along the pavement and then bounced into the wall of the shop. Something was wrong, he decided, as he listened to the chime of the village clock. The shop should have been open fifteen minutes ago. So he went up close to the shop window and peered through the many notices that were stuck to it, and through the many bottles of sweets displayed there in the window, to see if he could discover what was happening inside.

As far as he could tell, the owner of the shop, Miss Newcombe, as neat as a new pin as usual, was simply standing there at the counter talking to the driver of the van. He was just thinking to himself that this was hardly good enough when a police car came tearing down the village street. It came to an abrupt stop immediately behind the parked van, and out jumped P.C. Smallwood, the village constable, who was *not* a particular friend of William. In fact, P.C. Smallwood scowled darkly at William as he went into the shop.

William knew now what must have happened. There had been a robbery at the shop. William made

no bones now about pushing his face as close to the
shop window as his nose would let him do. It was then
that he realised that the trays of chocolates and the
bottles of sweets which were normally on the counter
were all missing. He could see Miss Newcombe talking
animatedly to P.C. Smallwood, her arms waving like a
windmill.

Without warning, there came a terrific snapping
and tearing sound followed by a soft soggy kind of
explosion. William turned so quickly in the direction of
the noise that he banged his nose hard on the wooden
frame of the window. Tears streamed in his eyes,
making it hard to tell what was going on. But after
brushing the tears away, William saw that both the van
and the police car now had all their doors ripped off, as
if by giant hands. The doors were simply lying there all
crumpled in the roadway.

"Hey, hey. What's all this?" boomed P.C. Smallwood.

"My van! My van! What's happened to my van?" moaned the delivery man in a high, thin voice.

P.C. Smallwood's hand tightened on William's shoulder.

"What d'you know about this?" he asked grimly.

"Nothing. Nothing at all," William replied truthfully.

"How can you know nothing, when you were standing here all the time?" the constable went on even more grimly.

The situation was saved by a shrill scream from Miss Newcombe. There was a new noise coming now from the shop, a noise like an enormous vacuum cleaner. William followed P.C. Smallwood quickly into the shop. To his amazement, not a bottle or a tray was to be seen. Just as the counter had been swept clean before, all the shelves were swept clean now and everything had gone also from the window. There was absolutely nothing left.

William was torn between curiosity and a desire to escape the attentions of P.C. Smallwood. Remembering it was curiosity that killed the cat, he decided to slip away. In the matter of slipping away, William was an accomplished master. In the merest flash, he was out of the shop. The van driver was standing there beside his van simply staring at it. With the back doors ripped off, William could see that the inside was completely empty. Just like the shop, the inside of the delivery van was bare, without a single sweet or a bar of chocolate to be seen.

William took to his heels, taking care to leave the main road for a path which led into fields surrounding the village, so that P.C. Smallwood couldn't catch him up in the doorless police car. He had just stopped for breath when a girl's voice said, "Hello there, you look terrible."

It was Kiryl, the daughter of the strange Professor Gamma. They lived in an equally strange old house called Wit's End, which was situated all by itself deep inside thick woods that lay below the Down. The Down was a broad hill overlooking the village.

"It is a morning of total disaster," replied William, still puffing to get his breath back. "Someone has stolen all the sweets in the village," he added, "so I couldn't buy my Neutron Bar."

"Neutron Bar?" frowned Kiryl.

"It's a new kind of chocolate bar," William explained somewhat testily.

"Why would anybody want to do that?" Kiryl wanted to know. "Go and look for yourself," growled William. "They've got the police all over the village."

"Then we'd better keep away from them," nodded Kiryl, starting off at a brisk walk along the track which led to a bridge over a stream, and then into the woods below the Down. William went along too, not quite knowing why he did so, except that something exciting always seemed to happen whenever he happened to run into Kiryl and her father.

In the wood they turned off the broad track they had been following on to a smaller track, and then after a while onto a still smaller track, which was hard to find unless you knew exactly where to look for it. The trees were now very thick over their heads, so that it wasn't at all the sort of place where you might expect to find a house.

Yet there it was at last, Wit's End. Whether it was because of the trees, or for some other reason, William had never been able to find the front door from the outside, although several times he had seen out of the front door from the inside.

He kept telling himself that the very next time he visited Wit's End he would settle the problem of the front door, but something always seemed to happen to make him forget about it. But now he remembered, and he was just beginning to look around, when Kiryl said in a testy voice, "Oh, come *on*, slow coach."

This was more than William could stand. He reckoned himself to be the fastest runner in the village and nobody was going to call him a slow coach. So he put on a burst of speed and beat Kiryl to the kitchen door of the house. The funny thing was that there never seemed any difficulty in finding the kitchen door.

Professor Gamma was sitting at a long wooden table with a magnifying glass in his eye. William could see that he had been examining the bowl of his giant pipe.

"Father," Kiryl said in a loud, clear voice, "something terrible has happened."

Gamma allowed the magnifying glass to drop out of his eye. Screwing up his purple-coloured face into a grimace he said, "Oh yes, and what might that be?"

"All the sweets and chocolate bars have been stolen from the village shop," replied Kiryl.

William hardly heard what was being said, because his attention was riveted by little specks of light that twinkled in Gamma's grey hair. Then as the professor banged the bowl of his pipe on the table the lights went out.

"Too many sweets and chocolate bars are very bad for your teeth, I would say," the professor remarked.

"But the doors were torn off the delivery van and the police car. How did that happen?" William managed to ask.

"Ah, that sounds a little more interesting. Tell me about it," said the professor.

So William described the loud ripping noise like a giant vacuum cleaner, while Gamma listened intently, with one of his eyebrows (the one where the magnifying glass had been) raised higher than the other one. To William's fascination, the twinkling lights came back into the professor's hair, at which Gamma banged angrily again on the table with his pipe, and the lights went out as they had done before.

13

Rising from the table, Professor Gamma went to a big wooden sideboard on which there was a very old-fashioned radio which had rows of tubes inside that lit up when the radio was operating. William watched the tubes begin to glow as Gamma pressed a switch, just in time for them to hear a special announcement: "Police

throughout the country are investigating a mysterious series of thefts of chocolates and sweets, centred it seems on a product called the Neutron Chocolate Bar. A spokesman for the Government says there is no cause for panic."

"Very interesting, very interesting," murmured Gamma as he switched off the radio.

"It sounds to me like a clever advertising campaign," Kiryl suggested.

"I rather think not. It sounds to me much more like my old friend Zuchario," the professor said in reply.

"Zuchario?" William asked.

"Zuchario, the universal sugar bandit," Gamma explained.

William would have liked to ask more questions but was prevented from doing so by the lights which appeared now quite dazzlingly in the professor's grey hair. At this, Gamma jammed the stem of the big pipe firmly into his mouth and by dint of puffing hard on it for a minute or two managed to blow out a thick cloud of smoke which filled the kitchen. Kiryl and William began to cough unbearably. Fortunately, Kiryl managed to open the kitchen door and gradually the smoke thinned as it billowed into the air outside the house. When it had gone, William could see the lights in the Professor's hair had also gone.

"That should have settled them," Gamma remarked with an air of finality. The only thing was, either the lights or the smoke had turned the Professor's hair a bright blue.

"The time has come to investigate, and we will begin by investigating the source of these Neutron Chocolate Bars," Gamma announced firmly, and led the way to a ramshackle shed where there was an old motor-bike with a side-car attached. William got astride the rear passenger seat and Kiryl into the side-car, while Gamma managed to start the engine after a great many kicks on the starter lever.

The motor-bike seemed to be just as old as the radio on the sideboard had been. The engine wheezed and clunked as they bounced along the narrow track through the wood. It seemed to be a long time before

they reached a good road, but once they were on the road a funny thing happened. William knew that the Neutron Bars were made in Birmingham, which was more than a hundred kilometres from his home village. Yet in almost no time at all, and even though the motor-bike seemed only to jog and wheeze along, they were there at the factory where the Neutron Bars were made.

There were many delivery vans, just like the one which had been at Miss Newcombe's shop, in the car park outside the factory. There was also a space marked VISITORS, and it was into this space that Gamma pulled the clunking motor-bike.

Just in time, for at that moment people started rushing in panic out of the factory doors. As they did so there was a ripping and tearing sound from all over the parking area. Metal doors crashing to the ground made a tinkling noise that was soon drowned by the rushing sound of an enormous vacuum cleaner. William could see a dark cloud being sucked up into the sky. It was only a few seconds before it disappeared completely, but in those few seconds William realised that the dark cloud was nothing other than an enormous swarm of Neutron Chocolate Bars. The mere thought of it made his mouth water unbearably.

Professor Gamma stood there scratching his blue hair and gazing up into the sky.

"If ever I saw an example of Zuchario's work, that was it," he said reflectively.

The sucking noise had stopped now, and everywhere over the asphalt of the parking area a heat haze began to develop. The air shimmered violently as flowing shapes of varying colours appeared about fifteen metres above their heads.

"Run for it!" yelled Gamma, leading the way with long raking strides to the shelter of a low stone wall which ran along one side of the car park. Kiryl and William were not far behind.

"What is it?" gasped William as he flung himself down on the ground beside the Professor.

"Zuchario himself, without a doubt. Take a look, but be very careful."

William raised his head carefully until he could look over the stone wall. There, hovering over the car park and over the factory, the flowing shapes were resolving themselves from coloured splotches of gas into hats of many different styles and shapes.

A bright red hat moved towards them. From it there came flashes of light and thunderous explosions which, in William's imagination, sounded like a gigantic bear growling out, "Zu-Zu-ZUCHARIO." The wall in front of them disintegrated, and the motor-bike began to glow.

"Time for action," muttered Gamma, taking aim with his pipe from which, with a whistling sound, burst a shape of light straight at the red hat.

Then a large green hat appeared around the corner of a building. From it there came a brilliant flash, and a car parked immediately on the opposite side of the wall slumped over as it lost one of its wheels. Gamma pointed the stem of his pipe in the direction of the green hat. William was almost deafened by a whistling sound from the pipe, as if an artillery shell had just been fired from it. Glancing towards the hat, he saw it vanish in a puff of green smoke.

A yellow sombrero floated over the wall from the direction of the chocolate factory, firing as it came. The Professor again returned the fire with his pipe, and the sombrero disintegrated into a delicate yellow cloud that blew quickly away in the wind.

William was just thinking that things were going pretty well when half the sole of his right shoe vanished. He looked up to see a black Homburg circling towards them. Gamma must have seen it too, for he swung his giant pipe around quickly and the Homburg disappeared.

The sucking noise like a big vacuum cleaner started up again. Through one of the gaps in the stone wall, which had been knocked out by the firing from the coloured hats, William could see box after box of chocolate bars streaming out of the factory. They simply soared up into the sky and vanished.

William noticed that although Gamma seemed to be disposing of the coloured hats, he wasn't really, for no sooner were they despatched in one form than they reappeared in another form. He could see that the yellow sombrero was back now in the shape of a deer-stalker.

There was a sudden shout from the Professor. "They've shot up my bike," he roared. Sure enough the motor-bike was entirely gone, except for one remaining wheel and the handlebars. "I'll have Zuchario's blood for this! That old bike was the apple of my eye," bellowed Gamma.

As if Zuchario had heard his threat, the firing stopped and there was a sudden silence. Then came the wailing of many sirens, as half a dozen police cars swept into the car park beside the factory, where they came to a juddering halt.

"I think we can now occupy ourselves better elsewhere," murmured the Professor, walking in long strides rapidly away from the factory, with William and Kiryl trotting at his heels. They had not walked far before they came to a large field, which surprisingly was completely bare.

"I'd have sworn something was planted there until recently," Gamma remarked as he gazed over the field.

"There was," came a voice from the other side of the hedge. "Until this morning that field was covered with sugar beet."

A burly man wearing a tweed jacket and a cloth cap, whom William realised must be the farmer, appeared from behind the hedge.

"Vanished, it did, the whole bloomin' field, about an hour ago," the farmer continued.

"What happened?" asked Kiryl.

"Dang me if I know. It just all went up into the sky,

as if it had been sucked up there by a vacuum cleaner," replied the farmer. Then he added, "But that doesn't make sense does it? Sugar beet can't disappear up into the sky."

The Professor resumed his rapid walk, leaving the farmer scratching his head in puzzlement. Gamma walked so rapidly that William began to wonder why he'd ever bothered to ride a motor-bike.

Eventually they reached a spot that was entirely out of sight of all houses, roads and people. There Gamma stopped and said, "The time has come to pay my old friend Zuchario a visit, and to teach him a lesson he should have learned long ago."

The Professor began to fiddle with his pipe, which William knew to be a communication switch that could project them into energy pathways which criss-cross the whole universe.

"Takes a little time to change the coding system, " Gamma explained.

"But why would anybody want to steal sugar?" asked William.

"Because sugar is vital to life," came the reply. "If Zuchario managed to strip the Earth of all its sugar, as he has done with many other planets, everything here would die."

"But what does he want with the sugar?" William persisted.

"Sugar is the most valuable commodity in the universe. There are some places that will pay anything to get hold of it," the Professor answered.

The adjustments to the pipe were apparently finished. Gripping the stem firmly in his teeth, Gamma gazed into space, the way he always did in the moment

before they dematerialised. There came a blaze of coloured light and William knew they were already far out from the Earth, edging themselves into the system of universal energy routes.

Dematerialisation never worried William. It was the materialisation at the other end of the journey which always frightened him a bit. On this occasion, however, the materialisation happened quickly, before he'd had time even to fret about it. Indeed it was the quickest trip into deep space he'd ever made.

"Straight through journey, no connections needed," explained Gamma, as they found themselves standing on the rim of a large crater.

Below them, thousands of arc lamps lit up what seemed to be a huge mining operation. Robot excavators and dump trucks were moving ceaselessly backwards and forwards, supplying some kind of material to a long conveyor belt.

"Interesting," grunted the Professor, taking off from the crater edge and beginning to run, slide and jump down the mass of rubble which formed the inside of the crater wall. William and Kiryl followed as best they could, with William in quite a lot of difficulty because he had only one good shoe.

When at last William reached the crater bottom he found Gamma examining a sample of the material which the robots were feeding onto the conveyor belt.

"Kimberlite," the Professor remarked.

"What does that mean?" grunted William, wishing that he hadn't banged his toes so badly in coming down the crater wall.

"It means that this place is a huge deposit of diamonds," Gamma replied. "Come on," he added, jumping onto a passing truck. Again with difficulty, William and Kiryl managed to follow.

They left the truck when it stopped beside the conveyer belt, getting off hurriedly before it dumped its load.

"What do we do now?" asked Kiryl in a rather fed-up voice.

"See where this goes," replied her father, full of enthusiasm as he vaulted up onto the moving belt. Once again, there was nothing William and Kiryl could do except follow.

The conveyer belt took them through tunnels and over embankments until it reached a very large building where millions of lights seemed to be ablaze.

"There doesn't appear to be much of an energy crisis here," remarked William.

"Not an energy crisis as we understand it," replied Gamma, "but I rather think we shall find quite a sugar crisis."

The belt took them into a vast hall. They climbed down and walked across the hall to a big door, through which they gained access to a whole series of similar large cavernous halls. In the last of them was a sight which made William suck in his breath and whistle, for on one side of it was a high pile of sparkling diamonds and on the other side a pile of glinting gold nuggets.

"Wow!" exclaimed Kiryl and William together in the same instant.

"Exactly so," nodded Gamma. "This is just what I thought we should find."

"But why would anybody with all this wealth need to steal sugar?" Kiryl asked in surprise.

"Exactly so," Gamma nodded again, clenching his pipe in his teeth. "This is why the situation is very interesting."

Another door led them into a huge silo, which William thought must be fifty metres wide and fully two hundred metres high. It was nine-tenths full of sugar of many kinds. More sugar was coming in all the time. "So to balance for what comes in, sugar must

also be going out," argued the Professor. "When we discover where it is going, our question will be answered," he added.

After some searching, they found a long tube into which sugar was disappearing. For a moment, William thought Gamma was going to jump inside the tube. Then with a sudden shake of his halo of blue hair, the Professor said, "I think not. Instead we will trace this tube. Wherever it leads, we will proceed."

The tube led them down a very long narrow corridor, blocked at the far end by a wall. The tube went straight through the wall, however, from the other side of which there came a continuous loud crunching noise.

"Just as well we decided not to travel inside the tube," nodded Gamma, smiling with satisfaction at his own good judgement.

"Father, have you any idea at all of what's going on?" Kiryl asked in an exasperated voice.

"Not really, but we are finding out. We are finding out," repeated the Professor in an unperturbed voice.

William couldn't see for the life of him how they could find out much more, because the wall ahead seemed completely blocked. But Gamma simply puffed on his pipe and a panel in the wall slid silently open.

"Nothing like having a complete set of skeleton codes," remarked the Professor with another satisfied smile.

The crunching noise grew still louder as they moved towards the opened panel. William followed reluctantly behind Gamma, because truth to tell he had no wish to encounter whatever it was that devoured the sugar so greedily on the other side of the wall. But to William's surprise the large room beyond was filled only with stack after stack of computer equipment.

"Is this the thing that's eating all our sweets and Neutron Chocolate Bars?" he asked in amazement.

"It would seem so," nodded the Professor.

"But I thought computers ran on electricity," William continued.

"Some do and some apparently do not. Electricity supplies energy, and so does sugar. There isn't any real difference," responded Gamma again.

A blue felt hat had come into the room, shooting as it came, but the Professor stood his ground coolly, firing from his pipe with a shrill whistling sound. The felt hat dissolved into a puff of smoke which was instantly attracted to one of the computer racks, on which it settled as a blue splotch.

"Here," the Professor said to William, handing him the pipe, "shoot at anything that moves, while I destroy the computer."

"How does the pipe work?" William asked.

"By thinking sensibly of course," Gamma replied.

So William gripped the bowl of the pipe, on the alert to fire at anything that moved.

A brown trilby hat appeared through a doorway at the further end of the room. The instant it appeared, William thought hard about Indians and Cowboys. To his astonishment the pipe gave a shrill whistle and the trilby dissolved into a brown stain on the floor.

There was another whistle, louder than the pipe, accompanied by a continuous "Beep – beep." Then a voice roared through the room with the cry "Intruders! Intruders!" A large white Stetson appeared, but William saw it and his aiming with the pipe was good, for the Stetson died with a dull "Ugh" sound.

The noise of the computer's siren, and the strange voice which kept on shouting "I'm under attack" got on William's nerves after a while, making it hard for him to concentrate. A shot from a deer-stalker hat hit the wall close beside his left ear.

"Wake up!" yelled Kiryl, tugging his arm.

The deer-stalker had dropped down among the computer racks. Every now and then it appeared around one of them to loose off a quick shot then duck away before William could manage to wing it.

But now there was a shriek from the computer, a shriek which died gradually into a loud moan.

"I'mmm unddder attaaa – – –" was the last that William heard from it.

Gamma appeared suddenly beside him, "All right, let's go," he said.

This was easier said than done, however, for with a noise which sounded like the drumming of horses' hooves, a red-feathered hat and a ten-gallon hat swept in among the computer equipment, pinning down Gamma, Kiryl and William with a fusillade of shots, to which the elusive deer-stalker hat also added its quota.

At this, the Professor took charge of the pipe again and opened up with such a barrage of heavy artillery that

William and Kiryl were able to slip away through the sliding door by which they had entered the computer room. They ran quickly along the corridor beside the tube that had supplied the computer with its sugar.

They could hear sounds now both behind and in front of them. Those behind turned out to be only Professor Gamma, who came up quickly with his long raking strides, but the ones in front had a metallic jingle, and they were heavy and deliberate.

"Zuchario himself, I'll be bound," growled Gamma.

The light in the large hall where the diamonds and the gold were piled high had been dimmed, which made it easy for them to see the red sombrero hat of Zuchario. The hat seemed to burn like a bright fire. Other coloured hats of all sizes and shapes were flocking to join it.

Then from the entrance of the hall came a furious drumming, just like the drumming of hundreds of galloping horses, and in the distance William could see a mass of dancing white hats. The Professor pulled Kiryl and William flat to the ground, just in the nick of time. Everywhere through the hall there erupted streaks of light and there was a noise like a continuous roll of thunder, so that to William it seemed as if they were in the middle of a furious storm.

Half opening one eye, William could see the red sombrero of Zuchario, surrounded by a mass of coloured hats. Every now and then one or other of them would evaporate into a cloud of smoke as they were hit by a streak of light from the white hats.

Suddenly the coloured hats surged out of the hall, to the loudest drumming of hooves that William had yet heard, and in pursuit of them danced the white hats.

"I rather fancy this should settle Zuchario's account for a while," said Gamma, rising to his feet.

The lights in the hall flickered and grew brighter, to reveal great empty holes torn out in the roof and walls by the violent shooting. William realised it must have been through one of these holes that Zuchario and his followers had made their escape.

Two bobbing white hats were coming towards William, Kiryl and the Professor.

"Thanks be to you, Strangers," a voice said, coming it seemed from one of the white hats.

"Is there anything more we can do for you?" Gamma responded.

Before either of the white hats could reply, William blurted out, "Why *was* Zuchario stealing our Neutron Chocolate Bars?"

A voice came from the second white hat, "Our planet was once very rich in sugar, and so we made the computer which controlled all our affairs to work on sugar. But the computer became more and more

greedy, until a time came when it demanded more sugar than we could produce."

"Why didn't you stop it?" asked Kiryl.

"We tried very hard to do so, but it was clever and it threatened to destroy everything, the whole of our planet, unless we met its demands for sugar."

"So you had to start buying from outside?" suggested Gamma.

"Exactly so, Stranger," went on the white hat. "But even then a time came when it became impossible to buy sufficient sugar from legal sources, and our planet became desperate."

"Is that why you went to Zuchario?" asked William.

"Yes. Zuchario was the only one who could obtain sufficient sugar to meet the computer's demands, which he did by robbing other planets of their sugar, leaving them bare, barren and useless," the first white hat explained.

"And you paid for the sugar with all this gold and all these diamonds!" exclaimed Kiryl.

Both the white hats dipped their hat brims in agreement. Gamma moved towards the entrance to the hall.

"We'll be on our way, now that everything has turned out for the best," he said.

"Oh, but you cannot leave without accepting some small token of our gratitude," exclaimed both white hats in a single voice. "Take whatever you wish."

"I know what I want!" exclaimed William, walking over to the conveyer belt where he could see a large pile of Neutron Chocolate Bars. But when he tried to scoop up a handful, Kiryl would allow him to take only one of them.

"It will be gone in a flash!" protested William.

Kiryl ignored William, and took just one chocolate bar herself, while Professor Gamma took just a small speck of gold which he placed carefully inside a white handkerchief.

The two white hats led them out of the hall, to a place outside where they could see what seemed to William like a normal sun-like star. Gamma nodded towards it and said, "Artificial, I think. It must have been the star which the computer threatened to turn off."

The white hats bobbed and weaved and again spoke in a single voice, "It was fortunate that you destroyed the computer before it destroyed our star." Then they were off, two white hats dancing into the distance to a noise that sounded exactly like the drumming of horses at a smart gallop.

"Home, and don't spare the horses," murmured Gamma with a grin as he began to puff away at his pipe. In a blaze of orange light they were instantly dematerialised.

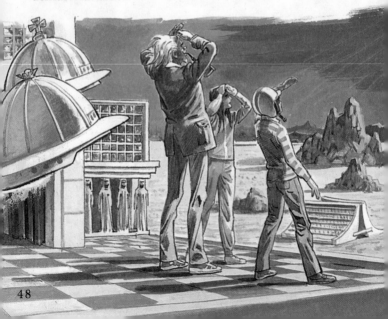

The journey back to Earth was faster than William ever remembered it from previous occasions. They materialised on the very top of the Down above his home village.

"Not bad shooting," remarked the Professor. "I was afraid that we would materialise at the chocolate factory, and then we would have had quite a long walk home."

"I'm sorry about your motor-bike," said William.

"So am I," nodded Gamma. "But next time I think I'll build one with four wheels instead of three."

As they made their way down the hill to the woods below, the Professor pointed out so many flowers and birds that it only seemed a minute or two before they reached a parting of their ways, with Gamma and Kiryl turning along a path through the trees towards Wit's End, and William making his way alone towards the village.

Suddenly he felt desperately hungry, so that there was nothing for it but to take a bite of his precious solitary Neutron Chocolate Bar. Although he tried hard to restrict himself to just one bite it tasted so good that he couldn't resist a second bite. Then he sternly wrapped up the remains of the bar in its paper wrapper and thrust it determinedly back into his trouser pocket.

Somehow he managed to forget about the Neutron Chocolate Bar until several hours later. When he eventually remembered it and took it out again he found to his astonishment that it was completely whole. Then he remembered that Kiryl had said he would need only one — because it was an indestructible chocolate bar that would always grow again, no matter how often he took a bite from it.